The Sock Animals Series #3

Sock Monkey's Family Reunion

For ordering information, see Resources section.

The Sock Animals Series #3

Sock Monkey's Family Reunion

Photography and story
by
Ann Jacobs Mooney

Library of Congress Catalog Card Number 98-92028
ISBN 0-9631035-5-5

First Edition 1 2 3 4 5 6 7 8 9 10
Printed in the United States of America

This book is dedicated to my parents,
Grace and Walter Jacobs, for giving me a
wonderful sense of family fun,
and to my husband,
Tom Mooney,
for helping me to create our own!

Once upon a time, there was a monkey made of socks. He had two sock friends, Tiger and Ellie the Elephant. These good friends played wild games of tag in the flower gardens, and always had fun.

The sock animals lived with a little boy who loved them all very much. But Monkey had been the little boy's first sock animal, and they were the best of friends.

One day, the little boy learned that his mother was going to have a baby soon. "I don't know yet if I'll have a brother or a sister," he told Monkey. The little boy was very excited.

Monkey was excited too, but he was also worried. What if the little boy was too busy with the new baby to play with Monkey? What if Monkey was no longer so special to him? Monkey tried to relax in his hammock and read his favorite book. But he was having some very worried thoughts.

The next morning, Monkey got an interesting letter in the mail. It was from his aunt who lived far away near the ocean. She was going to have a sock monkey family reunion and she wanted Monkey to come! Monkey packed a bag and told the little boy he'd be back in a week or two. He waved goodbye and off he went!

After a day or two, Monkey could tell he was getting close to the ocean. The air smelled salty! Monkey saw a sock frog chatting with an orange cat in the sun near a cottage. They both looked up as Monkey came over to meet them.

The cat was shy and quickly ran away. But the frog was very friendly. Her name was Frieda and she invited Monkey to visit for a while.

Monkey told Frieda all about his friends Tiger, Ellie, and the little boy. Frieda was such a good listener that Monkey even told her his worries about the new baby.

Suddenly Frieda saw her old friend Soctopus coming out of the ocean! She brought Monkey over to meet him.

Monkey, Frieda, and Soctopus quickly became good friends. Monkey had such a good time that he stayed for days.

Finally he said he must be on his way to the sock monkeys' reunion. "I'm so happy to have two new special sock friends!" he added.

Frieda asked, "Do you still care about Tiger and Ellie?"

Monkey was surprised. "Of course I do! Why did you ask me that?"

Frieda smiled. "So if you have new friends in your life, your old ones stay just as special as before?"

"Well, of course!" Monkey replied again.

Soctopus smiled, too. "I think you just taught yourself a lesson, Monkey!" he said.

Monkey thought about this for a minute. He understood that new friends hadn't changed his feelings for his old friends. So maybe a new person in the little boy's life wouldn't make Monkey less special to him after all!

Now Monkey smiled. "You're right, Soctopus. I just learned a very important lesson!" He gave Frieda a big hug and thanked her for her help.

Then Soctopus hugged Monkey goodbye with all eight arms! "What a great hug!" laughed Monkey. And off he went to the reunion with a happier heart.

At last Monkey got to Auntie's cottage by the ocean. He found her out in the garden. Auntie **ran to him** with open arms!

She was so happy to see him! They talked for hours. At bedtime, Auntie said, "Sleep well, Monkey. The reunion is tomorrow!"

That night, Monkey could hear the ocean as he fell asleep in a tent behind Auntie's cottage. In the morning, the warm sun woke him. He looked out the door of his tent and what did he see?

Monkeys everywhere!

The reunion had begun!

Monkey went over to Grandpa, who was sitting with his youngest grandchild, Monkette. Monkey loved chatting with Grandpa. "Do you know, Monkey, that I have twenty-seven grandchildren now! And every single one is so amazing to me." He bounced Monkette on his knee and she giggled. "I could have twenty-seven more and still love them all as much!" And Monkey knew that was true.

Then Monkey met his cousin Braidy. She was a teenager. Even though she was much taller than Monkey, Braidy and Monkey looked very much alike.

Monkey had fun meeting so many different monkeys. That afternoon, Monkey and some of his cousins went down to the beach. They talked and swam and laughed. Most of the cousins lived with boys and girls, and they all had wonderful stories to tell.

"Enough talking!" shouted the tiniest monkey. "Let's play!"

The happy monkeys leaped and tumbled all over the beach. They pretended they were seagulls swooping over the waves to look for fish. Then they jumped and slid down banks of slippery eel grass.

Suddenly Monkette ran out on the jetty of rocks that went out into the ocean. She slipped down between two big rocks.

Monkey ran over and pulled her up with his strong tail. After that, Monkette stayed right by Monkey's side for the rest of the afternoon.

At the end of the day, the tired monkey cousins lay down on the jetty rocks and watched the sunset. Then they walked back to Auntie's cottage to visit with all the other monkeys.

Later that evening after most of the monkeys had gone, Monkey and Grandpa were having a long talk. Monkey told Grandpa all about the little boy. Grandpa smiled wisely. "Your little boy has a big heart! He'll love that new baby too, but you will always be his very special monkey. And now Monkey, will you help me with a worry that I have?"

Grandpa said that Monkette wanted to live with a little girl or boy. But Grandpa had not been able to find just the right home for Monkette. "She is still very little. I want to find a very young child who could grow up with Monkette." Of course Monkey thought of the perfect answer to Grandpa's problem.

Early the next morning, Monkey found Auntie picking flowers outside. He thanked her for inviting him to the wonderful reunion and left for home.

Days later Monkey arrived at the little boy's house. A tiny baby girl had been born while he was away at the reunion. The boy was happy with his sweet new sister. And he was very, very happy that Monkey was back home! "Come and see my sister," he said.

They tiptoed into the baby's room. She was just waking up. Monkey told the little boy that he had a present for the new baby, and then Monkette jumped out of Monkey's bag! She ran right over to meet the tiny baby who would become Monkette's own special little girl.

So Monkette had her new home, and Monkey's and Grandpa's worries were all gone. Both Monkey and the little boy were happier than they had ever been before.

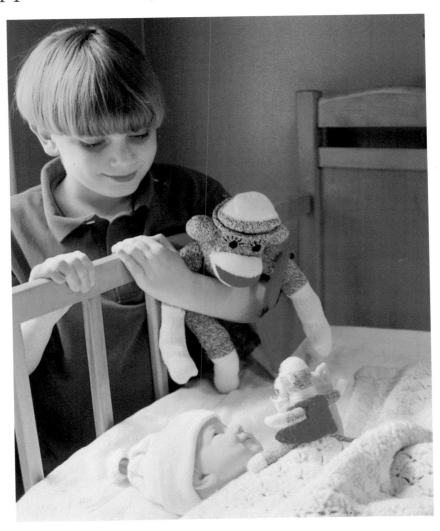

The End

Resources

These companies make products we used in the creation of animals for The Sock Animals Series. We appreciate their support!

Jamondas Press

Post Office Box 3325
Ann Arbor, MI 48106

Look for *The Sock Animals Series* books and gift packs in quality bookstores, craft stores and catalogs. They also may be ordered directly from Jamondas Press.

Tiger's New Friends
This storybook includes a section with directions for making Tiger, Monkey, & Ellie the Elephant.

Tiger's New Friends Gift Pack
This specially wrapped package includes the storybook with directions & one pair of red heel socks to make one animal.

Tiger's Vacation
This storybook includes a section with directions for making Tiger, Jake the Rattlesnake, & Hobby the Horse.

Tiger's Vacation Gift Pack
This specially wrapped package includes the storybook with directions & one pair of red heel socks to make one animal.

Sock Monkey's Family Reunion
This storybook includes a section with directions for making Monkey, Frieda the Frog, and Soctopus.

Sock Monkey's Family Reunion Deluxe Gift Pack
This deluxe package includes the storybook with directions, one pair of red heel socks to make one animal, & one pair of "mini" socks to make one baby animal.

We also sell the socks separately. For pricing or to place credit card orders, call our toll-free line: 1-800-223-7873.

Acknowledgments

I want to thank the following people who helped in so many ways to bring this book to completion:

Steve Maggio, for his cover design and great diagrams of animals;

Lisa Climer, for her consultation and helpful proofreading;

Walter Jacobs for his beautiful gardens that were the setting for the cover photograph;

Grace Jacobs for testing out Frieda and Soctopus prototype instructions in their early stages;

Carol Duvall and her staff for their enthusiasm for sock animals (The "Carol Duvall monkey" which I had presented to her on her television show appears in this book as "Auntie.");

Bob Folsom for loaning back to me the elderly monkey which I made him for his 40th birthday (This monkey appears as "Grandpa.");

Scott Mooney for being willing to keep his old-fashioned haircut to be "the little boy" in my book;

Tom Mooney for his consultation, proofreading, and ongoing support of this project;

Danny Mooney for his help in setting up various pictures;

All my friends and relatives who loaned props and helped with proofreading and setting up pictures; and

The Atlantic Ocean, particularly at Duxbury and West Dennis on Cape Cod, Massachusetts, for providing wonderful settings for my monkeys!!!

Ann Jacobs Mooney

Directions for Making

Monkey

Frieda the Frog

Soctopus

MONKEY

Materials

• One pair of red-heeled socks • Stuffing (polyester fiberfill, nylon stockings, etc.)
• Trim: black embroidery thread, buttons or felt (optional) • Red yarn (optional)

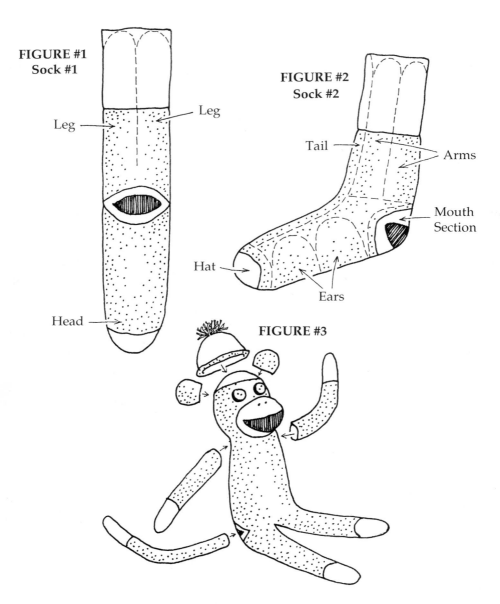

FIGURE #1
Sock #1

Leg — Leg

Head

FIGURE #2
Sock #2

Tail — Arms

Mouth Section

Hat — Ears

FIGURE #3

Please read ALL of the instructions before beginning to make Monkey.

BODY AND LEGS: Cut sock #1, making center cut stop about 1 1/2″ before you get to the white heel section. Stuff the head and body sections. Turn legs inside out and seam each leg, leaving crotch area and feet areas open. Turn legs right side out; stuff. Finish seaming the crotch. Decide how long you want the white ribbed foot area. Some people like small white sections for feet, while others leave all of the white ribbed section on. Trim if you wish, and seam the foot areas.

ARMS: Cut the upper part of sock #2 into two arm pieces. Again, decide how much white ribbed section looks good for the "hands" area. Most people make the arms shorter than the legs, so you may want to trim off 1″ or 2″ of the white section of the arms. Turn inside out and seam, rounding the ends. Turn right side out, stuff, and attach the arms.

FACE: Cut the heel from the second sock, leaving a brown edge around the white. Folding edges under, fasten it on to the lower part of the face, whip-stitching around the bottom. Stuff and finish sewing around top. Running a stitch of either black or white across the middle of the lips completes the mouth. Sew dark stitches for nostrils. A tie of yarn or heavy thread may be used around the neck to make the head area rounder.

EARS: Cut ears from the second sock as shown in Figure #2. Turn them inside out and sew a seam about 1/2″ from the edge, leaving bottom open. Turn right side out, stuff, and attach.

EYES: Sew on eyes: use buttons, felt, or embroider with black thread. (For young children, embroider eyes, as buttons can be pulled off and become a choking hazard.)

TAIL: Cut a 1″ strip (double thickness); taper to end in white cuff section. Turn inside out and seam. Turn right side out, stuff and attach.

CAP: (Optional) Cut off toe of sock #2, leaving 1/2″ of brown to roll for a brim. Red pompom can be added to top.

TRIM: (Optional) There are many variations of this basic pattern. Remember that for very young children, decorations that could be pulled off should not be used. But for older children, decorations can be either pompoms, yarn or bells. Jackets, vests and skirts are also used for Monkey's clothing.

Directions for Making

FRIEDA the FROG

Materials
- One pair of red-heeled socks, size medium • Stuffing (polyester fiberfill)
- Red embroidery thread

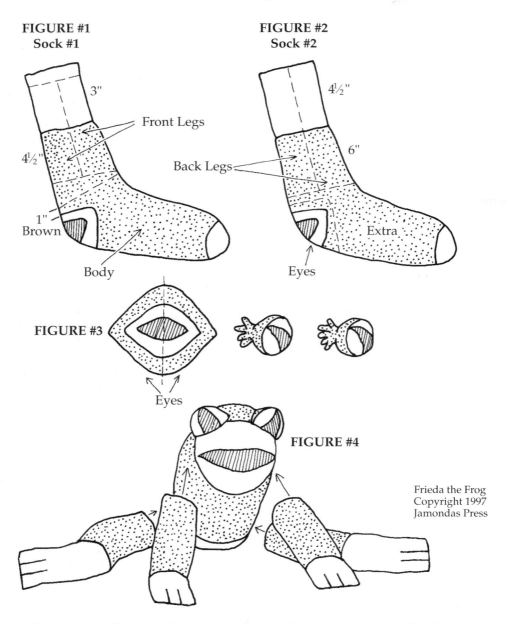

FIGURE #1
Sock #1

3"

Front Legs

$4\frac{1}{2}$"

Back Legs

1"
Brown

Body

FIGURE #2
Sock #2

$4\frac{1}{2}$"

6"

Extra

Eyes

FIGURE #3

Eyes

FIGURE #4

Frieda the Frog
Copyright 1997
Jamondas Press

Please read ALL of the instructions before beginning to make Frieda.

EYES: Take the heel of Sock #2 and cut it in half as shown in Figure 3. Take one half and put a running stitch through the outside edges. Put stuffing in the center, pull it into a ball, and sew it firmly into a ball shape. This will be an eyeball. Make the other half of the toe section into the second eyeball.

BODY AND HEAD: Use the foot of Sock #1 for the frog's body. The red heel of this sock will become the frog's mouth. Stuff frog body fully, including the mouth area. Position the eyeballs above mouth so that the red triangle of each eye has the tall point at the top. Place the eyeball so that the white part just touches the white over the red mouth. Fold under about 1" of the loose brown material over the eyes. Pull it down over the top of the eyeball so that the whole red triangle shows. The brown flap over the eyes will also come down to meet white of the mouth for about an inch or so between the eyes. Add desired amount of stuffing in the head; then sew eyeballs and flap in place. Take a few tucks in the brown area behind each eye so that each eye area has more of a round, ball-like shape. To flatten the head out, take a few stitches through the head, going in under the chin where white hits brown and going up through the area where the brown flap is sewn down between the eyes. This gives Frieda's head a broader, more frog-like appearance.

FRONT LEGS: Take one of the shorter legs from Sock #1. Fold wrong sides together. Seam by hand or on sewing machine. Sew white end shut (with square corners) but leave brown end open. Leave about 1/2" unsewn at the brown end of the seam. Turn inside out and stuff. Stuffing in white end should be fairly thin so you can flatten it out; leg (brown section) can be stuffed full and round. Do the same with the other front leg.

FEET: To produce the toes, use red embroidery thread and stitch two lines all the way through the foot, so that you have the red lines on the top and bottom. This makes the foot flatter and makes the toes look more delineated. You may have to take two or three red stitches in the same place to make the red stand out. Next, you need to make the foot bend out from the leg. Where the white turns into brown, pull the brown down about 3/4" over the white in the front half of the leg, and stitch it in place. This will make the foot angle out. Do this to the foot of the other front leg. Attach the front legs to the body about 1" back from the white of the frog's face. Front legs should hang down with feet pointing forward rather than to the side.

BACK LEGS: Take the longer legs, cut from Sock #2. At the edge of the white section (which will become the ends of the toes), trim off the end that has elastic thread through it. This will help the toes lie flatter. Make them up just as you did the front legs: seam, stuff, add toes, and sew foot at an angle. Since these legs are longer, the white foot area will also be longer. Attach these legs at the back of the frog, right where the brown body turns into the white rear end. When attaching the back legs, face the feet out to the side, rather than forward as you did with the front legs.

Frieda should be able to sit up with back legs out to sides and front legs propped up under the front of her.

Directions for Making

SOCTOPUS

Materials
• One pair of red-heeled socks, size large • Stuffing (polyester fiberfill)

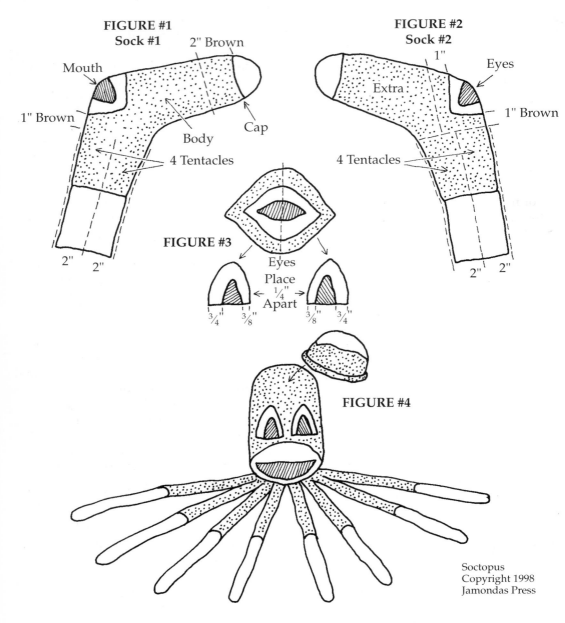

FIGURE #1
Sock #1

2" Brown

Mouth

1" Brown

Body

Cap

4 Tentacles

2"   2"

FIGURE #2
Sock #2

1"

Eyes

Extra

1" Brown

4 Tentacles

2"   2"

FIGURE #3

Eyes
Place
← 1/4" →
Apart

3/4" 3/8"   3/8" 3/4"

FIGURE #4

Please read ALL of the instructions before beginning to make Soctopus.

Tentacles: Cut Sock #1 according to Figure 1. Put the toe section aside for the cap. The remainder of the sock is the Soctopus's body. Cut the elastic edge off the top of the white cuff. From about 1″ beyond the white part of the heel up through the white cuff, there will be four long strips that will dangle from the body. Each of these will be a tentacle, and before being sewn, each will be about 10″ long and 2″ wide. Cut the same part of Sock #2 into 4 more tentacles; these will be cut off of Sock #2, about 1″ from the white part of the heel.

Read this whole paragraph before making the tentacles; some hints can save you time! Turn each tentacle inside out and sew about ¼″ in from the side edge and across the bottom edge. Sew either by hand or by machine. Since the sewn tentacles will be thin, turning them back right-side out will be a challenge. It is easier to leave a spot about half-way up the tentacle open for a couple of inches so that you can turn it right-side out in two stages; leave this gap open until after you've stuffed each leg to make the stuffing stage easier as well. Then simply whip stitch the gap up when the tentacle is all stuffed.

For the four tentacles that are part of the body sock, sew them each to within an inch of the top of the tentacle. Do not sew the top sections together with the other body-tentacles yet.

For the four unattached tentacles, sew each one right up to the top. Then join all four together at the top. The joined area will not be visible so it doesn't need to be fancy, but it does need to be solidly sewn (children tend to swing things with long limbs!).

Body: Stuff the body section, and sew the open top of Soctopus's head closed. Take the sewn-together set of four tentacles from Sock #2, and put the top section up into the bottom of the Soctopus's body. Folding under any raw edges, sew the inside four tentacles to the outside four tentacles very solidly.

Eyes: The eyes are made from the heel of Sock #2. The heel should be cut with about a 1″ margin of brown around the white section. Open the heel up, and cut it evenly down the middle so that you end up with two red triangle sections in the middle of either half. The heel on body sock is Soctopus's mouth. The two eyes you've cut can be placed about ½″ above the white of the mouth. Decide where you like the look of the eyes; some people like the eyes placed right down against the white of the mouth. Look at the pattern for the specifics of how much white to leave on the eyes when you fold back the brown margin. Then sew the eyes partly in place across the bottom; the extra brown material you folded under will partially stuff the eyes so that they puff out. Before completely sewing each eye on, add fiberfill stuffing to puff the eye out fully. The eyes should be about ¼″ apart.

Mouth: To make the red-heeled mouth puff out, sew several stitches from under his chin up through the mouth, catching the stitches up on the top of the white section of the mouth between the eyes.

Cap: Take the toe section of Sock #1. Roll the raw edge up so that there is about 1″ of brown before the white toe begins. Then sew the cap onto the top of the head to complete your Soctopus. Enjoy!